# Kidnapped in Mexico

## Contents

# Kidnapped in Mexico

# Preface

It was a beautiful morning and Thomas decided to pay a visit to his friend, Zack. Zack was a famous international soccer player, who was on the Brazil team, and he wanted to wish him luck before the FIFA world cup. FIFA was a very big tournament, and he wanted his friend's team to win.

As Thomas walked out the door, he smiled, "What a beautiful day today! Because the weather is so nice, it really got all the people out of their houses!"

It took Thomas at least an hour to get to Zack's house and he didn't even notice the house until he was right in front of it.

"Whoa! If that's Zack's house, I'm going to faint!" Thomas uttered.

He didn't want to faint but he rang the doorbell of the humongous, black and white house anyway. Zack answered the door, said 'hi' and watched as Thomas fainted.

# Chapter One: Is That A House, Or A Hotel?

After he woke up, Thomas realized that he was lying on a bed, in a giant living room. He could only see the ceiling, figuring out that the person who lives here must be super rich. Just in a few seconds, Thomas realized where he was and, after standing up, he was greeted by a friendly looking man and it is Zack.

"Great, you're awake! How are you doing buddy?" Zack asked.

"I'm fine, except I'm a little bit woozy from the fall." Thomas said, a little bit tired but he managed to hold back a yawn.

"Don't worry, you're all right. Why'd you come? You know that I'm really busy right now, with the FIFA cup and all sorts of stuff." Zack said.

Thomas smiled a bit, "I just like to pay you a visit and wish you a good luck for the game."

# Kidnapped in Mexico

Zack laughed and said that he would like to offer Thomas a tour first at his house. With much curiosity, Thomas asked Zack, "When or how did you get this giant house?"

Zack responded, "I got the house not too long ago; actually, just a few months old! I designed and built it with the soccer team, and the idea is we can all hang out here once in a while."

Zack continued, "I live in this house and so does my Sub, David, and he fills me in if I get a red card or a big injury during the soccer game. We practice together and we became good friends."

Zack pointed to the man that was watching TV and then Thomas examined him.

"That's David?" Thomas asked.

"Yep." Zack replied, "That's him."

Since he is a friend to Zack, Thomas went up to him to shake hands, but just before reaching him, something told Thomas not to. It was either the huge scar down the left side of his face or it was his gangster looking face.

While waving to David and waiting for a gesture or a reply, he never got one. At that moment, Thomas sensed that he would have trouble becoming friends with this guy.

"Okay, hello to you too!" Thomas said, in an awkward tone.

Afterwards, Thomas and Zack played all sorts of sports, like bowling, soccer, basketball, pool, cricket, tennis, and then went swimming. After all these exercise, Thomas felt exhausted, so he rested for a break.

"Woo! What a work out!" He said, but still wanted to play, "Let's play another game!"

They played four more games and, as it getting dark outside, Thomas begged Zack to let him stay longer.

"Can we play a different game?" He asked, whining like a three year old.

"Sorry, Thomas, you'll probably have to come another day, as you know tomorrow we have soccer practice and I have to invite the team, but I'll try to find a time to go somewhere later."

Thomas sighed, said goodbye, and then walked out the door. As he was walking away, further and further until the huge mansion was only a dot on the green grass. As soon as he arrived at home, he settled down and went to sleep straight away.

## Chapter Two: Zack, Kidnapped?

The next morning, at 9 a.m., Thomas received a message from Zack, "Hi Thomas! I found a time to go to Mexico, we could go this Sunday. I've already got the plane tickets and let me know if you could come!"

Thomas grinned, "Mexico! I've never been there!" he thought, and immediately called Zack. On the phone, Thomas was talking as fast as a cheetah could run, which pretty fast.

"Hey! Zack, I've received your call about going to Mexico. Of course I can come! I have plenty of free time! But wait, didn't you say that you had soccer practice? You finished all your classes earlier? Wow, you're such a great friend."

Thomas hung up and started packing. He sang a song while doing it, "Mexico, Mexico, what a country, it's like paradise, only smaller!" "Mexico, Mexico, only smaller!"

He laughed and called Zack again to thank for invitation to go Mexico. After waiting for quite a while, a wave of relief washed over him as Zack answered the phone, "Hello? Who's speaking- Aaahhhhh!" Then he heard the sound from the other end,

13

"Help, help me!!!" And the sound of chocking grew fainter and fainter in the phone.

Thomas laughed, "Come on, Zack, you can do better than that; I know that you're just playing with me!"

But then the line went dead...

"Hello, hello?" Thomas yelled into the phone several times, but no one answered. Thomas had no choices but to hang up and started believing what had just happened: "What if somebody kidnapped him?" He wondered aloud.

He decided to take a look himself, so rode his bike to the mansion without any delay.

"Zack, Zack!" Thomas shouted as he pounded on the front door.

The door was answered by Zack, "what happened on the phone? I thought that you got kidnapped!" Thomas said anxiously.

Zack looked to the left and to the right hesitantly, then he laughed, "Ha! You fell for it! You fell for it! I faked it and tried to get your attention!"

Thomas eyed Zack suspiciously, "Are you sure you didn't get kidnapped; are you Zack or you are his twin?"

"I'm not either."

"I tricked you, some detective you are!" Zack responded.

Thomas assumed something wrong with Zack, but he couldn't figure out what's exactly wrong. He shrugged and told Zack that he was really frightened and suggested that Zack shouldn't trick or prank him anymore. Thomas also mentioned that he was really happy for being invited to Mexico and so excited to see what amazing wonders there were in Mexico. After he said his farewell, he left for home.

As soon as arriving home, he continued packing and, when it was done, he was so tired and went to sleep straight away. In that night, he dreamed about Zack being an evil scientist, cloning himself in an experiment and then laughing as he understood that his result was positive. The evil laugh woke him up, he jumped up in bed, and put his hand on his forehead: it was soaking wet.

"It's just a nightmare, nothing to be afraid of." he said to himself, but inside he was freaking out and starting to think that Zack was really an evil scientist in disguise. Finally he decided to plot a stake out on Zack's house. It was time to figure out who Zack really was: an evil scientist or an awesome soccer player?

"Let's do this," he said, as he strapped his rapid fire Nerf gun around his back. "Okay, the Nerf gun may be a little too far but it makes me look cool," he said, while looking at the mirror. Then he ran out of his house and crept up closer and closer to Zack's house.

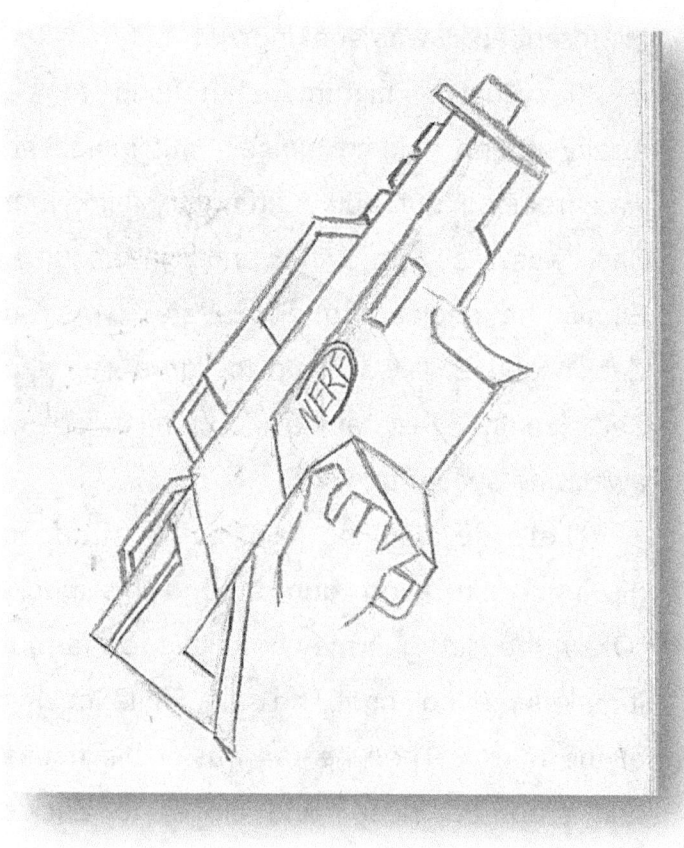

## Chapter Three: Suspicion

"Almost there!" He said, encouraging himself to go faster.

Finally he made it and plopped himself right below the window from Zack's room. It was downstairs, so he didn't have to worry about climbing the wall and hanging on the windowsill.

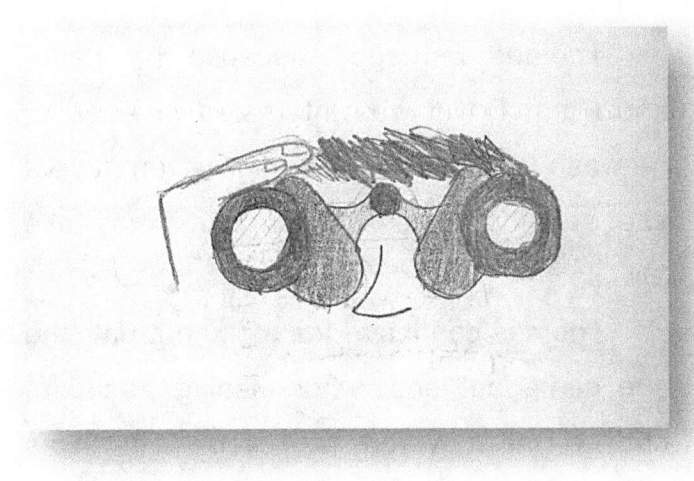

While looking at the window and trying to see what was going on inside the room, he saw Zack sleeping on his bed, looks like he was talking. After looking at the desk, he was scared out of his wits when he saw a collection of test tubes and notebooks.

"Oh my gosh! He really is a scientist!" After looking at the desk again, he started laughing as he saw what was on the note beside the collection. "Wait, the note says: *to David, please accept this gift from your partner, Zachary.*"

Thomas shrugged because he never knew that David was interested in science; he was wondering that he might even have a shot at being friends with him, but it may take a while.

Thomas continued the stake out until the sun came out and, when seeing Zack got change, he covered his eyes. "That was strange," Thomas thought, "Zack was normally sensitive about himself and would always bring down the blinds when he was going to change."

A short while later, Thomas opened his eyes but realized that he was a little bit too early; Zack still hadn't out on his shirt. One thing also surprised Thomas: Zack had a tattoo! As far as he knew, Zack never had a tattoo before, but things can always change, what if he just got it yesterday?

While watching Zack the whole day, he noticed it was as if Zack really did get cloned! Everything that he knew about Zack had changed: he knew that Zack was the best player on his team, but today, when Zack was trying to deke David out, he tripped on his ball and fell on his nose.

Furthermore, when it came to Zack's piano practical session with the teacher,

Thomas first covered his ears, as generally speaking, Zack's play was awful.

"Stand back everyone, the bomb is about to explode!" Thomas said, forgot he was hidden behind. Zack might've heard what Thomas was talking about because he walked right up to the window and opened it. Then he stuck his head out and yelled, "Come out, come out wherever you are hiding!"

Zack looked down, but couldn't see anyone, and then he walked away. Thomas was hiding in a bonsai bush and he didn't know that Zack was gone until he heard the piano. Thomas expected to hear a mixture of high notes and low notes, creaky sounds and freaky sounds, but instead, what he heard was something beautiful and sweet, "Wow! Zack has really been practicing and improving significantly!" Thomas thought.

He listened some more and, around an hour later, his class was over and the teacher said to Zack: "I must congratulate you, Zachary; your performance has dazzled me! I hope you play like this every day!"

After hearing what the teacher said, Thomas laughed, "Nope, that performance is one in a million!"

Again, Zack stuck his head out to see where the voice from, but could see no one around, just the bonsai bush and grass. At the end of the day, Thomas crawled out of his bush and walked back home.

When thinking about today's events, he questioned why Zack was getting better at piano and worse at soccer: maybe he spent more time on piano and his skills for soccer were fading away. Thomas even heard Zack sigh when the coach told him to have extra classes and to improve soccer skills.

*Does that mean no Mexico trip?* But hold on, when heard the dates of practice, he jumped in joy. If the last day of practice was a day later, Zack wouldn't be able to come to the trip.

Thomas knew that he was fortunate and it was a wonderful blessing. With the good news, he skipped all the way home in delight. He was imaging that he going to have a great time in Mexico.

## Chapter Four: A Book For Pickpocketing?

Following day, Zack and Thomas packed up to get ready to go to Mexico. Zack drove Thomas to the airport and then they waited for instructions.

Once they got onto the plane, Thomas was waiting for Zack, as he was in the airplane washroom, but took an extremely long time. Thomas thought that he may be doing a number two or just a real long number one, otherwise not so long. Thomas started reading an article, which he kind of took from Zack's bag, but he knew that Zack wouldn't mind. The title was also very interesting: "How to master the arts of stealing and pickpocketing."

To Thomas, this seems to be weird, but he kept reading it anyway. He read about the author and how he interviewed robbers in disguise as their boss. He also read about the amazing stunts that they pulled without getting caught, stealing huge time savings, and pickpocketing in front of a security camera. After two years of talking to a fake boss and spilling your secrets to him, at the end you ended up in jail, with no money and no hope.

At the end of the book, there was a picture of all the robbers that he tricked in jail. Thomas laughed at the picture as it was so funny, but something else flashed in Thomas' head. It was a newspaper that he remembered from a long time ago, talking about a professor who was killed and stabbed, in which there was a picture at the bottom of the title and it showed a familiar looking man that he knew. It was the professor who wrote the article that he was reading about right now.

Thomas automatically remembered what happened: he was in his arm chair and reading the daily newspaper. On the front page there was an article talking about the professor and his murder and, at the end, they had found the person who killed the professor: it was the robbers that the author had sent to jail. Unfortunately, the robber's sentence had expired and they plotted some revenge on the innocent man. It was sad and tragic but Thomas didn't pay much attention to it.

When the airplane landed, Thomas started dozing and woke up. He looked around, trying to make out where he was. He finally realized that he was on the plane flying to Mexico. Thomas climbed off, urged Zack to go faster and shortly they were in the Mexican airport.

It was super busy but Thomas didn't notice a thing: he was controlled by all the lights and colors. They leaded him out the door and onto the ground faster than he had expected. Thomas and Zack met each other at the entrance and then started looking for a hotel that was nice and cozy, also suitable for them.

They found a good one, close to airport and, as soon as arrived the hotel, they were overjoyed, immediately unloaded their bags and started diving onto the beds. They played "hide and seek" in the humongous room and nobody ever got caught. When it was time to go to bed, they jumped on their beds until they started missing Gravity. After getting exhausted, they both went to sleep and soon started dreaming.

## Chapter Five: An Attempt To Take Zack And Thomas' Lives!

At some point in midnight, Thomas woke up at a shuffling sound and, when looking around, did not see Zack in his bed. He rubbed his eyes and stared at his bed, trying to make Zack appear.

"Zack? Where are you?" Thomas asked, eager to find if he was safe and sound.

"I'm over here, in the washroom. I'm shaving." Zack responded.

Thomas shrugged and went back to his dreams. He had the same dream about the crazy scientist and cloning stuff. Because of bad dreams, he was tossing and turning and never got any real sleep until four in the morning.

Once he got up, Thomas walked over to the phone and ordered his favorite food, spaghetti! He wasn't Italian, but he just liked the taste of spaghetti. And one of his favorite things from spaghetti was the sauce and the meatballs, served round and juicy, which really yummy.

While waiting for his food, he watched a movie with Zack. It was funny and sad, but it was alright. The food arrived when they were watching the movie, which often caught Zack staring at the spaghetti and drooling. Thomas was not sure if Zack liked spaghetti, but you may never know as things always change. Thomas once hated lollipops but now he would lick one any chance he got.

After finishing the spaghetti, Thomas left it on the table, thinking that the room service staff would clean it and bring it to the kitchen. He went out for a walk and looked at the insects like butterflies and dragonflies. While walking around, he saw some moths and caterpillars.

Meanwhile, he was thinking about that phone call, the one Zack sounded like he was getting kidnapped:

- It was too harsh! Why would anybody try to kidnap Zack?
- Zack was nice to anybody he knew! Once he even saw Zack stop a gang of big kids bullying some first graders!

When thinking of those cute, small kids, Thomas smiled. They were so funny and, when they thanked Zack, they looked like they believed that Zack was a superman.

As thinking about the phone call of Zack's kidnap, he just shook the idea out of his mind. He continued walking and suddenly heard an explosion from the direction of the hotel.

Thomas turned around and started running, "If that was in my room, I could at least thank God that I got out of the mess!"

He hurried into the hotel and saw that the first floor was completely deserted. While wondering if anybody got hurt, he decided to use the stairs to go up and, when got on the floor, he froze in shock as he saw his room:

- It was on fire, and Zack was inside it!

"Zack...!" Thomas yelled, hoping that Zack got outside the room before the fire to practice playing soccer outside or doing something else.

"What is it?" A voice said from behind Thomas.

Thomas turned around and saw Zack! "Oh my Gosh, I was so worried about you, Zack!" He was relieved and hugged Zack, and then they watched the firemen while they taking out the fire.

After the firemen did their job and left, Thomas and Zack stared at the black room in shock, "That's going to be a lot of money for our cleaning bill." Zack muttered under his breath.

He took pity on Zack: *his life almost ended in that room and all he cared about was a silly cleaning bill!*

Thomas explored the whole room, testing his foot onto the ground before taking a step. The floor was solid but you could put your entire hand through the wall and into your neighbour's room. He actually felt someone's hair as he stuck the hand through the burnt wall.

Thomas pulled his hand away quickly and heard a really high scream from the other room. Frightened, he still chuckled and started looking for his belongings. Surprisingly, on the wooden table, his bag was safe and sound. The same goes to everything inside it.

With some puzzles, Thomas pulled out his phone, clothes, toothpaste and toothbrush, some books, pencils and notebooks. He threw the notebooks out as he never needed them. Thomas saw the TV remote on the sofa and it was also a bit fried, but when he pressed the ON button, the TV turned on!

Quite surprised by what he found, Thomas was too happy to care: the TV was the only thing that he had right now. He continued watching cartoons for the rest of the day, while Zack was playing on the computer.

When the time comes for their sleep, Thomas went to bed but jumped right up once he felt the bed sheet and blankets.

"Whoa! These beds are so spiky!" he claimed, "Where are we going to sleep now?"

Thomas thought that the manager was going to sort this all out, but he never showed up. Much worse, the manager even said that he never knew his own hotel was on fire. The fact is, when Thomas called him, the manager told him that, when got the news, he was very nervous and scared.

*This might be another mystery to solve for him*, Thomas signed.

# Chapter Six: Seriously, Again?

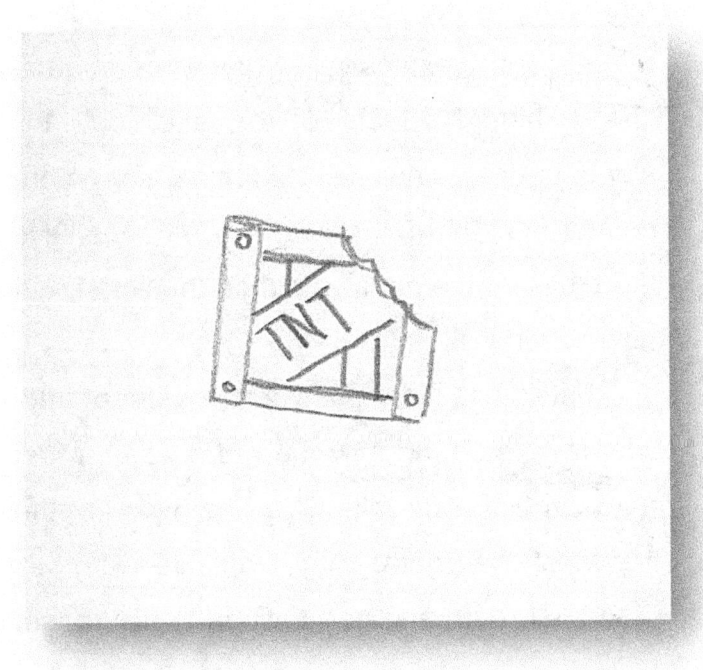

When searching the room, not too long after, he found out that someone snuck an explosive stuff into their room. There was a box marked **TNT** and he knew that, if searching more, he would probably find the trigger for the explosive. As it was getting too late, Thomas decided to take out his sleeping bag and slept in it, which more comforting than the burnt up beds. He thought that the beds would be the worst, but he was wrong.

Later on, Thomas went to sleep and, when woke up, he saw the room was on fire, once again, but this time, he was in the inside of the room, rather outside. Thomas held his breath and got down onto his knees. He started crawling and then picked up his sleeping bag and dragged it to the washroom.

## Kidnapped in Mexico

After soaking the sleeping bag in hot water and putting it over his body, he opened the door and crawled out the room. Thankfully, he was safe and not burned!

Thomas sighed and looked at the room, "That's the second time we had a fire. And it looks like Zack made it outside in the nick of time, again."

Speaking of the fire, Thomas was thinking about Zack and how he always gets out of the room and never shows up when the fire erupts. He started suspecting Zack for the two fires, but shortly shook the idea out of his head.

"It may just be a coincidence, nothing to worry about." He thought.

With the fire in his mind and no any delay, Thomas called room service and they came up with the firemen in a few minutes. He also asked the people in the front where Zack was and the manager said that he left an hour ago to explore the wonders of

Mexico. He believed what the manager said and decided to go out to look for him.

"Zack, where are you?" Thomas screamed, "Come out, Zack, come out wherever you are!"

He was looking for Zack everywhere and finally found him at one of the tourist gift shops.

"Zack, where did you go? Our room caught on fire again!" Thomas asked.

Zack stared at him and then laughed, "You're joking, man; right?"

"If our room caught on fire, how then you

survived?" he continued, "You're so funny, Tom!"

Since Zack did not believe what he said, Thomas just turned and walked away; if he insisted, Zack might thought that he was mocking him. After leaving the hotel, he could still hear the laughter from the hotel.

Thomas started thinking about it, "Zack would never buy anything from a rundown, rickety and old gift shop!" "So what's going on here?"

He wondered that Zack might've changed his perception recently, but anyway, maybe just leave like that. Thomas went to ask the manager to see if they can get another room. The manager agreed, but warned that he was in a danger.

After hearing what the manager said, Thomas didn't believe that, or ever thought about it, but something inside told him to listen. After got the key and went into the room, he attached the Wii console into the TV and started playing video games.

Thomas played Mario kart 8 and some other racing games. He liked them and wanted to learn how to drive the car someday. It was his dream to drive up and down the streets of Toronto and, even better, speed through the highways until he had no more gas. He smiled and thought about himself in a Ferrari laughing, and even smiled to himself.

## Chapter Seven: Robber!

While thinking about his future, suddenly someone broke down the door and, without a second hesitation, Thomas jumped in fright and turned off the Wii.

He caught a glimpse of who broke into his room; it was dressed in black and had one of those ski mask things that normally robbers would wear. Thomas held his breath again,

- Robber!

Thomas snuck toward the front door and hid on top of the refrigerator. He didn't know how he got up there, but it might be he was really scared, thought that the robber was coming for him, and just did a magic jump.

He was watching as the robber stuck his pistol in front of him and kind of waving it around. Thomas held his breath and on purpose dropped a glass vase onto the floor in front of the robber.

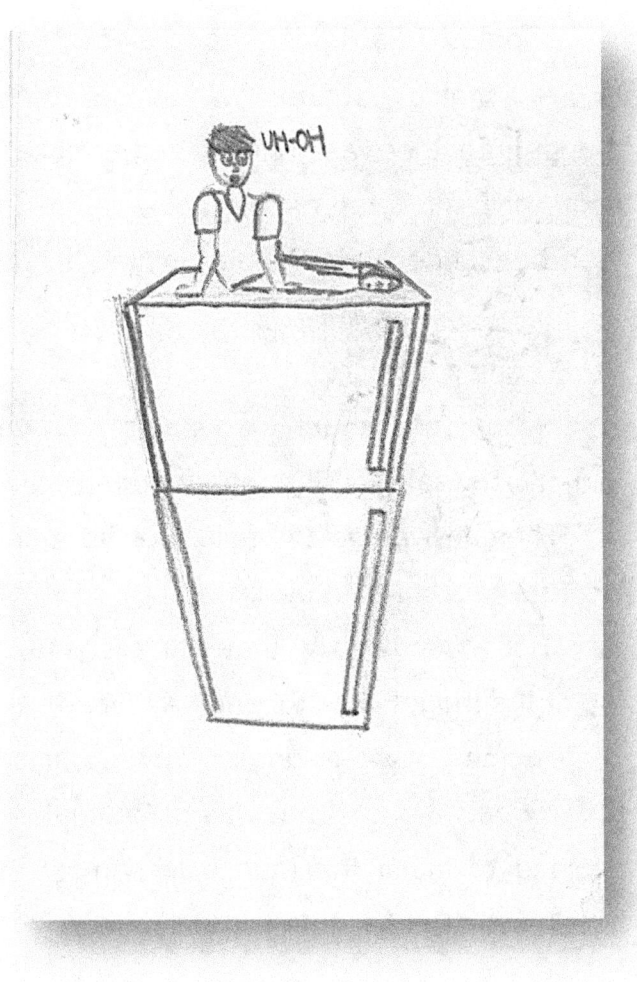

The robber jumped and yelled, "Mamma, Mia!"

Thomas heard his strong accent and realized that the robber was an Italian. He dropped another vase, closer to the robber's head, and snickered as the robber jumped in fear, but suddenly the robber pointed his gun at him.

Thomas was frozen!

"Whoa, check out that statue, Mamma Mia, it's so realistic!" the robber grumbled.

Thomas wanted to smile, but he didn't. He knew a lot of statues like that.

"But I wonder why they put a statue on top of the fridge!" The robber mentioned.

Thomas was thinking to frown, but still the robber thought he was a statue! He decided to teach the man a lesson, so he tipped over and fell onto the Italian man.

## Kidnapped in Mexico

The robber yelled again, "Mamma Mia!"

Thomas landed right on the top of the robber's head, grabbed at his curly hair, and started pulling.

"The statue's alive! Alive, I tell you, alive!" the robber frightened.

The man grabbed at Thomas, but Thomas bit his hand off, and spit on him, thinking that the man needed to clean his hands. Thomas dropped all the hair that he ripped out onto the floor and, less than a minute, the robber became bald.

Thomas jumped off the man and punched him in the groin with full strength. The robber walked backwards, grimacing in pain, and then Thomas caught the falling pistol.

# Kidnapped in Mexico

"Surrender" Thomas said, pointing the gun at the man's chest.

Five minutes later, the policemen came and handcuffed the robber. The man struggled with them, but no match for the troop of fifteen policemen.

Shortly afterwards, the robber was taken away and, while Thomas waving good bye to him, the robber stared at him, and he was turning red and really mad. Thomas laughed and believed that the man was really weak and had no experience.

## Chapter Eight: The Gift

After all these, Thomas thought about Zack and wondered when he was going to come home. Since no much to do, he started playing video games and, later on, he went to bed and soon the dreams started.

In the middle of his sleep, Zack came back to the room and put something under Thomas' bed, which is a box with a red ribbon at the top. After leaving the box, Zack smiled and then went to sleep on the new bed. "Tomorrow, Thomas is going to have a big surprise," he thought.

Thomas woke up early next morning and, for some strange cause, couldn't get back to sleep, so he decided to take a walk outside to explore the streets of Mexico.

He rode on a tourist bus and saw a bunch of stores, entertainment rooms and lots of people laughing. Thomas donated at least twenty dollars to the hobos on the street, and felt bad for them, because while watching the men and woman so happy and glad, they were on the sidewalk begging for money. He thought that everybody who sees a hobo should donate at least one dollar, which will lead to a happier life, and then there would be no more hobos on the street.

In one of the souvenir shops, Thomas saw a very nice present and decided to get for Zack. After exploring the city, he took a tourist bus back to the hotel and put it under his own bed, waiting for the right moment to give it to him. Meanwhile, he saw the present that Zack put under his bed,

"What's this?" he wondered aloud, "it looks so awesome!"

Thomas walked to the window and saw the wrap was open. He didn't mind, and started opening the packaging, but noticed a bird poop on the package.

Taken by surprise, Thomas yelled, "AHH!!!" and the present dropped down the air.

He was trying to lunge for it, but since he was on the highest level of the building, he was too scared to fall to his doom.

"There goes my present." He whispered.

Too sad for both, Thomas originally thought not to tell Zack about what happened and just pretended that he never found the present. But after thinking one more time, it wasn't nice to lie to one of his closest friends, so he decided to tell the truth, but exaggerate a little bit.

When Zack woke up, Thomas told him the story like this, "Umm Zack, I need to tell you something; this morning, I found your little present that you hid under my bed." he continued, "but maybe I opened the package too close to the window, so it dropped."

Then he cleared his throat, "it was a tragic to see the present land on the sidewalk and explode."

While waiting for his answer, Zack nodded and turned around, "I need some private time." then he left the room.

Feeling ashamed, Thomas wanted to comfort and tell him that it was okay, but he didn't want to upset Zack even more, so he just let Zack go and have his own 'me time'.

While starring at the door for several seconds and snapping out of it, he remembered the present that he bought. Thomas took it from under his bed and put it under Zack's bed. He played more video games and watched more TV.

When Zack was back, Thomas was eating his lunch, noticing Zack holding his arms behind his back. Thomas suspected that something was wrong with him. "I wonder what he's doing!" He thought.

## Kidnapped in Mexico

Thomas was watching Zack suspiciously as he eating the meal, and then he heard a sound of something landing on the carpeted floor, but he thought that it was just something from next door.

He didn't ask Zack about the 'arms behind the back' thing because he was thinking to solve the mystery by himself, but it seems to be impossible and too complicated, so he gave up and walked up to Zack. When almost reaching him, suddenly Zack turned around with a smile, holding a box in his hands, "Surprise!" He yelled at Thomas.

Thomas jumped up in shock, seeing the box opened automatically, in which there were two pieces of paper inside. He read the one that was addressed to him, "Cineplex, the Lego movie."

Such a surprising gift, Thomas thanked Zack and shook his hand several times before letting go. He always liked Lego, but never knew that Zack did too!

When the times came, Thomas and Zack ran to the theater as if they were being chased by an evil witch, minus the screaming and screeching. As soon as arriving at theater, they immediately chose their spots and sat down.

Thomas loved it already and asked Zack if he could buy a slushy, even though he knew the answer was going to be "No". But to his surprise, Zack agreed, so he jumped up and made a mad dash to the lobby.

"I'll be back in a jiffy!" He called at Thomas.

Thomas nodded and continued watching the pre-film show. Just before he finished watching the commercial of 'How to train your dragon 2', Zack landed in his spot on the left hand side. He smiled and took his blue slushy. Thomas slurped the slushy the whole time and laughed when Zack got annoyed. When Thomas emptied his cup, he asked for a refill.

Again, at second time, Zack agreed. Thomas thought, "That sounds strange, as Zack normally doesn't like slushy."

Thomas emptied his cup again and, this time, he didn't ask for a refill and the plan was to get Zack to refill the cup without asking. If Zack did it spontaneously, he would have to believe that Zack has a new hobby for buying and refilling slushes.

Again, this time, he couldn't believe his ears and eyes as Zack asked him a single question, "Oh, Thomas, I see that you're cup is empty, you're drinking a lot of slushes today! Let me refill that for you." Thomas agreed to let him go and shrugged.

"I guess he does have a new hobby," he thought, "That is a really weird one."

When they finished the movie, in total Thomas had drunk ten slushes! That night, he went hotel with Zack and, on the car, he decided to get some shut eye, but after arriving hotel, he wasn't that tired, so he watched the news and went to play video games. Later on, when got tired, he walked to his new non-burned bed and jumped on it.

Thomas expected that he was going to fall asleep very quickly, but for the whole night, he just kept tossing and turning, and his eyes even not closed for a second. The scene was on his mind and he kept on thinking about the two fires and the robber. He heard the robber say somebody's name, and it sounded something like, "Denel" but he wasn't too sure.

## Chapter Nine: Goofing Around

When thinking about the stuff that happened, Thomas speculated that somebody may be threatening him.

"No, impossible, I'm all the way here in Mexico! How could anybody know I'm here? Maybe the fires and robber were just a coincidence." He wondered.

Finally, Thomas went to sleep around one o'clock in the morning and woke up at seven. When got up from the bed, he noticed that dark circles around his eyes. He mumbled as walking to breakfast table and slouched on his chair. Definitely, he was not in a good mood. He only ate one piece of toast and drank one glass of milk.

Afterwards, he still wasn't happy. When it was the lunch time, he ate some spaghetti and felt a bit better; maybe magic spaghetti make a day for him. He sat on the couch and watched some programs on TV. On news channel, he saw a report about a fire and a robbery.

He was thinking to turn off the TV, but something inside told him to leave it on. Maybe it was himself or he was just too lazy to reach for the TV remote. He continued listening and heard a familiar name, "Thomas!"

He smiled, "I think I know that person! He's... Myself!"

Gasped in amazement, he was surprised to learn that he was on TV!

"How did they know that he got robbed and almost caught on fire? Are they either psychic or really smart?"

It might be a good idea to visit the news centre and to learn how they operate, so Thomas decided to pay a visit to the news station.

"Zack, I'm going to the news center!"

No answer!

"Zack, Zack!"

Still no answer!

# Kidnapped in Mexico

"It was him! It's Zack who told the news reporters about the fires and the robbery! That traitor!" Thomas was getting a little upset.

Shortly, Thomas stomped right up to the news station and didn't care when several men and women talked about his attitude and behavior, probably only a few people noticed who he is. He heard some people talking about him:

"Isn't that Thomas, the famous boy detective?"

"Look, mama, that boy is mad!"

Thomas grumbled to them and, when walked inside, he was shocked by all the lights and shiny cameras.

"What? But how is that possible?" Thomas heard some people saying.

"Cut!" a reporter walked up to Thomas and scowled at him.

Just judged by his face, Thomas predicted one thing: *this isn't going to be good.*

Thomas backed away and regretted coming here. "What are you doing here?" The reporter studied Thomas' face and then suddenly covered his mouth in shock,

"It's you! You're the boy detective! You sent the robber to custody!" He immediately started shaking Thomas' hand up and down.

Thomas didn't understand, "Uh, thanks, I think?" he replied, surely not understanding this man's attitude.

"Can I have your autograph?" Thomas shrugged but didn't give it to him.

"Do you mind if I could see the room where they're casting my story?" Thomas asked.

"Yes, sure, whatever you want, Sir." The reporter led Thomas outside and onto the street.

# Kidnapped in Mexico

Just in front of him, Thomas saw a happy looking Zack and really getting mad.

"It was him!" He thought.

Thomas walked away from the man and into the reporter's camera. Thomas was now on TV and everyone watching the news was confused by the intruder, but the reporter didn't look puzzled. He played along as if everything was planned out like this,

"And we have a few questions for the young man that is the hero of the story." Zack gasped and Thomas smiled.

"So, Thomas how do you feel after you fought the two fires and the robber? You seem like you don't know a thing!" The reporter said.

"What robbery? What fire? Sorry I am not sure what you're talking about. My friend over here is a huge jokester, but I do know someone who helped me catch that robber." Thomas motioned for Zack to leave and laughed as he saw the reporter's face once Zack was out of the camera's view.

Thomas called a taxi, seeing a worried looking Zack jumped in as well. Thomas shook his head in shame as the two of them were going back to their hotel. He felt bad for ruining Zack's moment of fame, but he didn't want too much attention. Three people already targeted him with two fires and a robbery. He didn't want anything else to follow.

Before this trip, Thomas expected that it was going to be awesome one, but from now, the only thing that he wanted to do was to go back home as soon as possible. He looked out the window and sighed.

When thinking about it one more time, actually this might be a good thing: you can't always have too much action! So Thomas smiled and finally decided to forgive Zack for whatever he did. It's still nice to have him at his side! He also really liked the slushes that Zack gave him.

Once seeing the hotel just in front, he fished out the money owed to the driver and then got out of the car. After giving the money to the man at the wheel and thanking him for the lift, he glanced at Zack and felt sorry for him.

*This was going to be a long trip!* He signed.

While on the way, Thomas never looked at Zack in the eye, and neither did Zack. They walked to their room separately and sat down in silence.

"I'm sorry." Zack finally broke the silence.

"I'm okay, it's just that I don't like any attention. If some random bad guys watching that channel and found out that I was a detective, they would suspect that I'm a threat. They'll probably target me and try to eliminate me. And you know that I'm not very fond of being killed."

## Chapter Ten: The Abduction

Later that evening, Thomas and Zack set up a security system in their hotel room, which was nearly invisible to normal people and only available to be spotted from the middle of the ceiling. Of course, there were lights, cameras, action! They tested the system and found it quite successful.

They were wearing earphones connected to the security, so whenever an alarm went off, it would go straight to the police and into their headphones. But there is a problem here, if the bad guys heard it, they would know that they were trapped and would run away, instead of being caught.

Thomas added the finishing touches like a see-through string at the doorway of their room. Whenever someone stepped on, it would sound an alarm, and describe the patterning under someone's shoes. Of course the alarm was loud enough to wake a koala from its sleep.

Thomas was careful of everything and didn't take any chances. If the bad guy was smart enough to dodge a trap, another one would just follow.

His favorite system was the remote control car, which has a mini camera taped onto its front and programmed to videotape any kind of human coming from the entrances. There were four of them guarding the windows and door.

Zack's favorite system is pretty dumb: at the peep hole, there was a black strip of paper and, in the strip of paper, there was a tiny mini hidden camera, which can take pictures of the bad guy's eyes. The hi-tech police said that the camera could trace the man by examining the eye.

After saying good night to Zack, Thomas put on his headphones and went to sleep, knowing that, with all the security system set up, he was safe and nothing going to happen to him. In the dream, Thomas had a hundred men grabbing at him, asking for his autograph. The most disturbing thing was the hands coming from the ground and they weren't actually hands; they were hands of skeletons!

He woke up in a flash after the skeletons climbed out of the ground, whispering his name, "Thomas, Thomas!"

Once waken up, he still heard the whispering and even felt the grabbing on his back.

"What?" This was getting creepy. He looked to the side and saw Zack gagged.

"Zack, where are we?" Thomas was getting really scared now.

He saw Zack turn his head to face him and then whispered to him: "We're kidnapped; don't try to resist; I heard where we're going and, here I'll tell you, we're going to.., OUCH!"

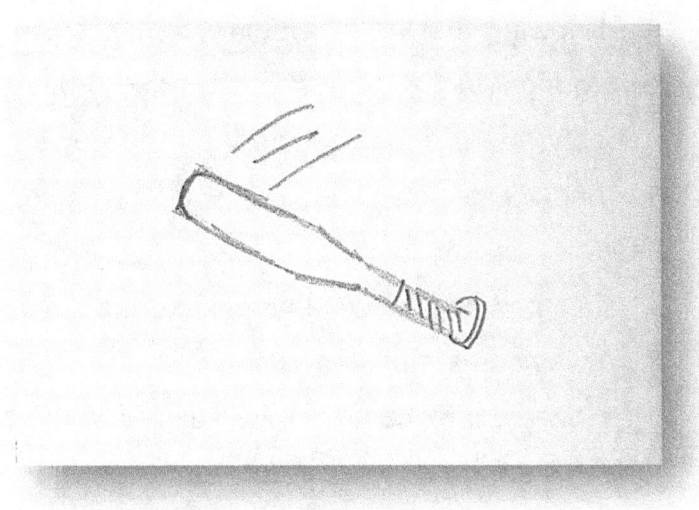

Someone hit a baseball bat onto Zack's head, very hardly. Zack blacked out and lied there, unconscious and without any move. Thomas thought it would be fine for Zack as he knew the location and how to get back.

Plus, Thomas didn't want to get hit by a wooden baseball bat.

Knowing that he was being carried by a few gangsters, he suspected that they probably heard about his story on the news. He tried to lie down, but still couldn't go to sleep.

Thomas sensed what was bothering him: there was something wrong!

How did they come in? He still lied in the burlap sack and wondered about all the security traps and really no idea how they got in?

Thomas thought to ask the gangsters later when they reached their destination.

"They must be very smart," Thomas thought and, soon, fell into sleep.

Now, you wouldn't believe that a boy like Thomas could sleep while in a burlap sack, being held by a bunch of gangsters. But he did and thought it wasn't so comfortable though. He wouldn't mind if escaped.

When woke up, he realized that he was in a cage, beside Zack, both handcuffed.

"It seems to be comfy here." Thomas thought.

When looking outside of his cage, he noticed that they were in a room, along with a lot of other prisoners, who sitting in other cages. Thomas looked at the closest cage to him, and recognized the person right away:

She was the president's wife!

"How come?" He wondered.

He then looked at the cage on the opposite side of him, "Say what! It was the one of the most famous soccer players in the world, Messi from Argentina!"

Thomas was getting excited that he was so close to his favourite soccer player, but he had to start acting serious. He nudged Zack with his elbow and asked him, "So, you said you knew how to get back to our hotel. Can you tell me how?"

Zack turned around and looked at Thomas, "umm, who are you and who am I?" He asked.

Thomas laughed, "Stop joking around! We have to escape!"

"It's funny, but I have no idea what my name is and I don't know who you are." Zack responded.

"Oh no." Thomas wondered what happened to Zack, "You must have amnesia!" He looked at the spot where the gangsters banged Zack and there was a big bruise on it.

"This isn't good." He looked at the bruise again, "How are we going to get home?"

Thomas tried to move around in the cage and decided that he would never let Zack go close to a reporter ever again. These gangsters have been smart enough to capture a lot of famous guys. If this keeps on going, who knows what might happen. The weird thing was Thomas knew nothing about this.

"The gangsters might have bribed the victim's family and friends to be quiet." he thought.

When looking at other famous people that he knew in the other cages, he noticed Jackie Chan meditating in the middle of his cage, whose steel bars were a bit dented and bent, so Thomas got some ideas of what he might be doing.

Zack was still trying to remember what had happened before he got knocked out. While looking around, Thomas noticed something that he didn't see before,

"Zack, do you know that everyone has a plaque that says the name, how much for their ransom, who kidnapped him, and when captured!"

"Come on; let's see how much we're worth."

Thomas walked up to the lock of the cage and stuck his head out the bars. He was actually surprised that he did that, because usually, if you were in jail and, if you could stick your head out the bars, which means you were fit enough to slip through the bars!

At beginning, he never thought it's possible for him to try that and, even if he could, he was too tired. After a few times of trying hard to see the plague, Thomas still couldn't see it properly, so he inched his head out a little bit more.

"How come these plaques aren't even visible to the person that it's licenced to?" Thomas pushed his head out a little bit more and then it happened:

- Thomas tripped and his head fell back and banged back onto the bars again; his head slipped and his body fell out of the cage!

"Oh yeah!" He shouted, all the other prisoners stared at him in shock.

"Hey Thomas, you're out!" Zack said.

Immediately, they too started stuffing their heads out. Thomas saw Messi fall out of his cage and celebrated, and then Jackie Chan's head butted the cage and spun in midair, landing on his feet in a crouching position, who said something in Chinese that Thomas couldn't understand.

One by one, the prisoners popped out of their cages, some actually came up to Thomas to thank him and wanted to ask for his autographs.

"Okay, no more autographs, we need to get out of here!" Thomas commanded.

"Yeah!" Everyone chorused.

It sounded like chaos from inside, but Thomas was more worried about the gangsters outside.

"If they heard us, we're going to be in big trouble," he thought.

"Okay, listen up! Everyone, be quiet, otherwise these gangsters will come in and lock us up in these cages again; in that case, we never got another chance!" Thomas said, in a half whisper, half shout. Right now, he looks like a leader, even in front of those stars.

"Everything would be going apart, except if we came up with some plans." He wondered.

## Chapter Eleven: Kidnapped In Mexico!

Thomas looked at his surroundings and thought that this place was very familiar. He tried to remember what bothered him as he watched the other men and women chatted to each other and made buddies. He noticed Jackie Chan breaking the cage bars and handing one to each person. The people decided to use them as weapons.

Zack remembered that he was a soccer player and he became friends with Messi. They were tall, light but very destructive.

While seeing everyone get along well, Thomas laughed, "I've got a good idea!"

He asked for everyone to come together for a team huddle. Thomas assigned them to the duties and instructed how they going to escape. He gave Jackie Chan and another strong looking man the duties for security.

If anyone came in, they would use their bars to knock them down. He asked people to find out how many gangsters in the building; they would take care of half the gangsters and later stampede out the door, charging with their metal bars and even maybe throwing some pieces of the cages.

When asking if everyone agree with the plan, he was surprised that they all agreed, "Nice plan! It's funny too!"

# Kidnapped in Mexico

Thomas grinned, "I guess, that means that everyone agreed!"

Immediately, each individual began readapting to their plan in a flash. By the time when a gangster came in the room to serve lunch, Jackie Chan tackled him down and the other man, who seemed to be a former soldier from war, knocked him out cold. They had a feast over their food and the high fived each other and thanked Thomas for setting them free.

What confused Thomas was that, "why didn't they think of this before?" "Weird, seems no one ever noticed!"

He shrugged and guessed that maybe they were too sad to even try. When Thomas asked another man that day about this question, that proves his prediction was right,

"We were just too worried that the kidnappers would hear us and penalize us. But after you did it, we waited a few seconds, knowing that no one came, we also ran out of our cages! Thanks!"

Thomas shook hands with him and then asked the people if there was anybody that wanted to come with him and spy on the gangsters.

"Me!"

"I do!"

"I'm an undercover policeman! I've got experience!"

Thomas was surprised by all the people that wanted to join, so he decided to make it easier and sort it out,

"Okey dokey, who is a policeman, or woman, please step over here."

Thomas had to step to the left to actually let the policemen and women have some space, and it turned out that nearly half the group were police!

"Okay, now if you have the experience, like you're from the army or a professional mixed martial arts artist, please step on the other side of the room."

He gasped when the rest of the room tried to squish them together at the back.

"This is harder than I thought!" Thomas shrugged and almost decided to go ahead with the stampede right away, but then figured out that it would be too dangerous if there were too many kidnappers; at first, they would have to find out how many kidnappers there were.

Thomas chose the spies among the people and concluded with fifteen men and women, ready to go on an adventure. Even though gradually, Zack started remembering his history part by part, he decided to leave Zack to stay with the other men, as he worried that Zack wasn't ready yet. He discussed the plan with the team and, once they all understood, they immediately got to work.

After an undercover policeman boosted him up to the air vent, Thomas unscrewed the bolts and dropped the bolts to the ground. After the team were in the vent, he told the other men to secure the bolts in place again. They agreed and soon everyone on the team got in the vent. Thomas used his phone as a flashlight and was actually delighted to have it.

"Maybe there's just no signal, so they letting us have our phones." He gasped.

They kept following the sound of deep laughter until they could see the gangsters. Thomas looked at his phone and realized that it was dinner time.

"Oh man, the gangsters are going to serve the prisoners now! Let's just hope that Jackie Chan does his job correctly."

Thomas almost jumped when someone tapped him on the back, "Umm, Mr. Thomas we need to go!"

He turned around and stared at the man behind him in shock, "What, but, aren't you supposed to be a security guard?" Thomas asked.

"Nope, you told me to come with you." Thomas almost collapsed, but kept on crawling.

"Where's the other guards?" Thomas hoped that the answer would be something good.

"Behind me."

Thomas sighed, "I hope they're going to be okay."

Thomas kept crawling and finally they found the kidnappers. He looked down and saw them. When counting all of them, he counted twenty. Thomas double checked and counted twenty again.

"Okay let's go." Thomas whispered to the front of the line.

He was now at the back and wasn't too fond of staring at someone's butt. He winced when he thought he heard a miniature explosion come from someone's rear end. Thomas didn't dare to smell the air and say, "Refreshing."

# Kidnapped in Mexico

He held his breath the whole way back. Breathing only from his mouth for the first few minutes, he couldn't stand it because he thought that the overpowering gas that was in the air was entering his mouth. Thomas didn't want anything like that to happen, so he just held his breath the whole time,

"How is this ever going to end?" Thomas held his nose in disgust, as the fart was loud and powerful.

While on the way back, he worried about the men and women at the jail house. Thomas wondered if the waiter caught them and reported them already. He urged the group to crawl faster; he elbowed the butt in front of him and gave it a hard push.

The man that owned the butt fell forward and did a front roll, pushed the man in front of him and soon, it looked like a game of human dominoes. When each and every man fell over, they stared at the back of the air vent, trying to see who did it.

It was Thomas who was at the back and who was easily blamed. Thomas smiled, shyly,

"Umm, can you go a bit faster?"

They grunted and got up, picking their pace to be faster.

"Phew." Thomas sighed; he thought that the generals and policemen were going to beat him up on the spot!

He started smelling the air once again and realized that the air smelled like lavender. The man in front of him noticed that Thomas was enjoying this new smell, so he pointed to his rear end and said,

"I started wearing air fresheners, which make my fart smell good!"

Thomas laughed, "So that explains the two lumps on your behind!"

They continued to crawl and, finally, when they reached the room, Thomas heard the man at the front yell into the room and ask for someone to open the vent. Somebody came and they heard a sound of metal falling onto the ground.

Thomas sighed, "Let's get out of here!"

He crawled out of the air vent and stretched out his arms and legs. He talked to the men that helped in the mission and the other prisoners started asking questions. Thomas answered them one by one, told them about the number of gangsters and, at the end, he noticed a person in one of the cages,

"Hey, I thought everybody escaped!"

The prisoners looked at the cage where Thomas was looking at and beamed,

"We caught the boss! He was coming to give us dinner and we used teamwork, I tackled him, the general knocked him out and the policeman put him behind the bars! You like?"

That surprised Thomas; maybe these people aren't so bad after all!

## Chapter Twelve: The Attack

By looking at his watch, Thomas realized it was night time. He told everyone to get back into their cages and start sleeping. He wondered if anybody would come in and realize that the waiter was missing. He didn't want to take the risk but, still, the prisoners complained, so Thomas sighed,

"Fine, I'll have first watch."

Everyone smiled, Thomas shrugged, and asked if anybody wanted to have second watch. He chose someone and the rest of the team went to sleep on their shirts or hats, used as pillows. Thomas held a metal bar and sat at the entrance, out of sight from people walking by.

Instead, some people wanted to sleep in the air vent, for extra safety. Thomas warned them about the green air, (a.k.a. fart) but they didn't listen.

"I guess you won't blame me when you come out in the morning asking for gas masks."

When checking his watch, it was almost eleven. Hearing someone coming, Thomas held onto the metal bar tighter and, when hearing the sound getting closer, he stood up on his chair and prepared for the attack.

He listened for the sound of footsteps and, when a head show up, he struck hardly by full force. The man yelled and fell down to the ground.

Waken by the scream, other team members all saw the man on the ground.

They beamed at Thomas and started to pull him into a cage. When that's done, it was Thomas' turn to sleep, and the other men sat on the chair and waited. He went to sleep, another day in the gangster zone.

After woke up, Thomas saw the men who went into the vent and their faces turned to green. Thomas laughed, "I warned you! But you didn't listen."

He started waking people up and telling them that the waiter was going to give them breakfast soon. They immediately awoken, ran into their cages, and the ones who had no cages went into the air vent, looking not so happy.

Thomas sat in his cage and spun it around, so it looks like the missing bar which they pulled out was invisible. While waiting for the food, Thomas never got any, nor did the other prisoners. He was puzzled and confused. They decided to stay in their cages until it was lunch time, but they didn't even get their lunch. Just taking another chance, they sat there for a little bit longer and waited for dinner, but never got any.

Everyone was starving and wondering what had happened. They asked Thomas, "Sir, why didn't we get any food? I'm dying!"

Thomas shrugged and replied, "I don't know, but I can check, who wants to go on an adventure?"

He waited for the hands to come up and glad to see them, so he chose the brave warriors from the team. A few of them came up with him and crawled into the air vent. Thomas plugged his nose and crawled with one hand, so did everybody else.

"Come on; let's see how much food they have; I'm starving!"

They crawled as fast as they could, each holding a metal bar in their pocket. They decided to ambush the kitchen and steal all the food, taking the gangsters back as prizes.

After a few minutes of crawling in the vent, they decided to unplug their noses, surprising to find out that the air smelled like air fresheners. Thomas kept on climbing and, finally, they smelled food. They took a deep breath and smelled the air, it smelled like chicken wings, salad, rice, potatoes and some ice cream.

When looking down at the room, Thomas saw the surroundings: all the men were sitting at the dinner table and realized that there was no security. He checked for hidden cameras and found there weren't any place to hide them. Thomas motioned for them to come closer and listen to the conversation,

"So, where's Bill? He should've been here last night!"

"Eh, who cares, he was the one responsible for the prisoners' food, and maybe he just doesn't want to feed them."

"If he doesn't want to give them food, let them starve."

After hearing what they talking about, Thomas got angry and his face turned red. The men knew what this meant, it was time to attack. Thomas broke open the air vent by kicking it, and the vent entrance fell onto the floor.

The gangsters all looked up and watched as the group of spies came down with their metal bars. They looked very scared. One by one, the men on Thomas' side knocked the gangsters out. They put all the food into a burlap sack that they found.

Thomas helped toss the gangsters into some more sacks and threw everything into the air vent. They pushed a sack until reached the prisoner room, where they held the celebration.

Everyone cheered for the ones who got the food and they had a small snack as Thomas suggested the team to conserve the food, so that it would last longer, but they probably not got the point and asked why need to keep food longer.

Thomas was worrying about the gangsters that were going to catch them, but then he realized that they already caught the gangsters, so nothing to worry about. They should have a big celebration and everyone deserves it.

After the team had a huge feast, they were all full and started looking the ways to escape. Everyone crawled out of the hide out and made way to the exit. They found pretty hard to find the exit; by taking left turns, right turns, elevators, eventually they found the exit.

## Chapter Thirteen: The Escape!

They walked out of the building and, eventually, came out with free. Now the first far more important thing is to find out where they were and, when looking around, they found themselves in the middle of nowhere. There was gravel and some fence, but it doesn't look like anything. They all looked back to the building that they were coming from and it resembled the shape of a barn.

Thomas said, "Surviving in the middle of nowhere, lesson one."

He advised to go out and look for a road. They figured out that, if they follow the road, they would find civilization. On the way ahead, they found a sign, "BEWARE KEEP OUT!"

The letters were drawn with some red paint, giving it a scary look. They kept on walking and finally agreed to split up: Thomas took out his phone and told someone on the other side to do the same.

Zack went with the other team and they started parting ways.

After a few minutes, Thomas realized something missing: they didn't give each other their phone numbers.

He told everyone about the problem, "Guys, does anyone know Jackie Chan's phone number? If we get lost, we won't have anyone to help us, so it would be kind of useful to call each other."

Thomas waited to see if anyone knew the number, but this is what he heard:

"I don't know!"

"Don't look at me!"

Thomas sighed and sent a man to run to the other group and get the information. He sent the man with his phone and instructed him to put the number into the contact, so he wouldn't forget. They waited for the man to come back and, eventually when the man came, he was sweating like a pig. He handed the phone to Thomas,

"His, gasp wheeze, number." Then he collapsed.

Everyone looked at him stunned and, a seconds later, he got up; everyone laughed, and they started to walk again. This time they had to wait for the man who got the number to catch up with them. They finally reached a fence and a road appeared on the other side. When looking back to the place where the barn used to be, they couldn't see it.

Completely disappeared!

They thought that the gangsters wanted it to be invisible, so that no one could see it. Thomas called the other group and a voice answered like,

"Hello, this is Boston pizza, how can I help you?"

Thomas laughed, "Wrong number."

Thomas was actually surprised that he called the pizza place as he thought it never had signal. He dialed another number and then Jackie Chan came on the phone.

He pondered, "Why couldn't he just have called the police?"

While trying to gather the whole group together, he got a call,

"Yes, hello? Is this Thomas?"

"It is me!"

"Yep, just to let you know, we've found a road. Just turn around and walk the way you've came from. Bye."

Thomas hung up and waited for the other group to arrive and, during the waiting time, someone suggested to climb the fence. Thomas thought it is a good idea, so did everyone else.

"Okay, I'll go first and see if it's safe." Thomas suggested.

He climbed up the fence and his back towards the group. Once he reached the top, he turned around, so he could see the men. He climbed a few centimeters down, and then jumped. He landed on his feet and dusted himself off,

"It's fine!"

The rest of the group climbed over and jumped off the fence. They too, dusted themselves off. Then they waited for the other group to arrive. They waited and waited, but no one showed up, then some of the men started to fall asleep.

At the end, the other group came. Thomas woke everybody up and they got together to discuss which way they should go. After some arguing, negotiating, talking and discussing, they decided to split into groups again.

They said goodbye, and then split up. Thomas' group were pumped and ready to walk as they had a long rest. Soon they started to see a bridge. Thomas saw a sign on the bridge that was blue and it had some white writing. Thomas ran till he could see the sign clearly,

"Express route."

He cheered up, "Hey guys! Check out the sign! We're on the high way!"

Thomas laughed and then ran back to the group. The group competed closer to the sign and then they slapped Thomas on the back,

"Good job buddy!"

"We're finally going to get back!"

Thomas, the Boy Detective

## Chapter Fourteen: The Lucky Break

While the group started skipping along the road, Thomas realized something, "Umm, guys you know how we said that we going to come back to the barn and capture them with the police?"

"Yeah," they replied.

"Well, if we don't remember the way, how are we going to find it?" Thomas asked.

"Easy, I know it by memory! Walk straight turn left at the sign, do a U turn, umm... yeah, I don't know the way."

111

Thomas sighed and they went to retrace their tracks. The group walked backwards this time and scattered metal onto the ground, instead of bread like Hansel and Gretel. They skipped and ran backwards until they got to the field.

"What a workout!" They followed their trail back, continued walking, and then it happened: a black Buick coming towards them!

Thomas jumped in joy, "Guys! Check it out! A car!"

They craned their necks up from looking at the ground and saw the car, "Woo hoo!"

They all started waving their hands wildly. When looking closer, they saw something shining at the top of the car: It was a siren!

Thomas couldn't believe his luck: It was a police car!

As they watched with the car getting closer and closer, the car came to a stop. The man in the vehicle pulled off his dark sunglasses and tipped his police hat, "How can I help you young man?"

Thomas blurted it out, "We were kidnapped! Kept in human sized cages!"

"We managed to escape the cages and run away!"

"You have to help us!"

# Kidnapped in Mexico

As the officer looks speechless, Thomas thought that the officer wouldn't believe them, but when the officer scanned his face, he recognized it at once, "Thomas? Well, now I totally believe you, and is that the missing general from the force?"

The officer continued, "Well, show me where the hide out is and we'll arrest those gangsters right away!"

The whole group relieved and, after a few minutes, they had found the field where the barn was. The policeman used binoculars to see the barn, "Yep, there it is. Right in the middle of the field."

They climbed over the fence and then started running until they reached the barn, and then opened the door.

The policeman took out his Walkie Talkie tool and asked for some back up. He put back the communication device, instead pulled out a gun, and then followed Thomas to the prison room without making a sound.

"It was this way." Thomas showed him the direction.

When almost going to go around the corner, suddenly, a sound of mad people and clanging metal came closer and closer to them.

"Get up! Get up!" Thomas said to the policeman, so they climbed up some coat hangers and up onto the ceiling. Thomas used some of his Invisi-spray, which was one of Thomas' latest gadgets, and sprayed him,

"Hey!"

Thomas motioned for him to be quiet and sprayed both of them. When looking into the bottle, there was still a lot of the liquid left. Very quickly and quietly, they climbed down to the ground and then stuck to the wall. While the angry gangsters were passing, they did not notice their existence.

Just for a fun or experiment, Thomas tapped the last man on the shoulder,

"Hey! Who did that?" Everyone looked at him.

"Did what?" They asked.

"Never mind, I must be losing my marbles." The man murmured.

Thomas and the policeman followed the gang of gangsters (or GOG for short). When the right time came, they attacked the gangsters: Thomas punched the man on the back really hard on a specific spot and then the man was out cold; the policeman was more experienced and he did a round shaped kick, at the same time three men falling to the ground.

The other men didn't hear anything, as the thumping of the bodies falling to the ground, and thought that it was just their footsteps.

"Come on, hurry up guys." The gangster at the front said, and continued walking.

Just before going out the door, someone said, "Did you hear that?"

The man turned around and saw the bodies on the ground, "Eh, maybe they are falling into sleeping." But surprisingly, they did not stop and kept on walking.

Thomas breathed a sigh of relief, "That was a close one." he whispered to the policeman.

He chuckled and they continued stalking the kidnapper. When it was the right time, Thomas tapped the man on the shoulder, but the Invisi-spray wore out, so the villain could see them now.

The gangster turned around and, when looking at Thomas, he grinned. When looking at Thomas' companion, who turned white as a ghost. The gangster whispered to the one behind, "Umm, boss?"

"Not now, Jeffrey." The man replied.

"Umm, it's serious."

"What is it!?"

"Turn around."

The boss turned around and gasped,

117

# Kidnapped in Mexico

"What!"

"Run!" He yelled, and they started speeding off.

Thomas and the policeman chased after; the man at the back threw his metal weapon at Thomas' head, and Thomas ducked. He ran faster, also mad that the gangster was going to escape. While turning around the corner and almost gaining on them, he pounced and grabbed onto the gangster's foot, "Let go!"

The gangster tried to shake Thomas off, but it was no use. He tried to punch Thomas, and Thomas deflected it by using the gangster's foot, so the gangster punched his foot and then fell down in agony.

While running after the other gangsters and seeing the kidnappers out the door, Thomas sighed, "They got away!"

However, the policeman was happy! "Not if I can help it!"

The gangsters got pushed back into the building's entrance, with handcuffs on their wrists.

Thomas gasped, "Wow! It's magic! How happened?"

Then, some policemen rushed through the door and shouted, "Down the hallway! Get them!"

The policemen ran after the rest of the bad guys and, after they caught and handcuffed the gang of gangsters, they gathered them all up. At the end of the commotion, they found the rest of the prisoners (that were captured by the GOG).

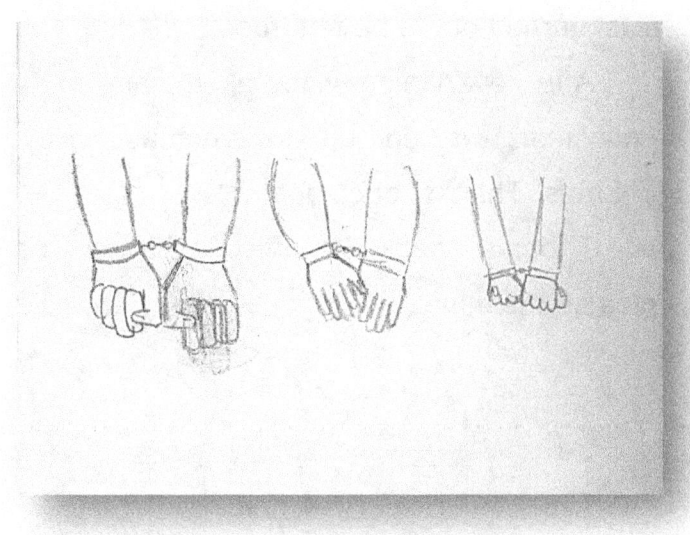

Thomas went to talk with Zack, "Umm, Zack, why were you acting so weird for the last few days?" he asked.

"Well, I don't know, I think it's that I got a few new hobbies!"

Thomas was relieved and the suspicious Zack turned out to be not true.

After everything was taken care of, a policeman walked up to Thomas, "Hey, Thomas, Thanks, once again!"

Thomas shook the officer's hand, "The pleasure is mine."

**About the author:**

Alex Chai is a grade-6 student, likes adventure, ski, and travelling. He was born at Edinburgh, Scotland, spent a wee bit time of his early childhood there. Later on, he moved to Palo Alto, California and, currently, lives at Toronto, Canada.

Alex likes jokes, and his favourite hobbies are reading, writing and playing sports. He hopes that he will write many more adventure books and thinks that readers will enjoy reading the story as well.

**About the publisher:**

**Panda Creative Publishing** is a place publishing books written by kids at all ages, and helping kids develop their writing skills. It provides a fun place and allows kids to express their imagination and cultivate curiosity by telling stories.